RATS IN THE WHITE HOUSE

BY JUDITH TABLER
ILLUSTRATIONS BY LEO LÄTTI

Printed in the United States of America

ISBN 9781735912707 (paperback)
ISBN 9781735912714 (ebook)

Canoe Tree
Press

4697 Main Street
Manchester Center, VT 05255

Canoe Tree Press is a division of DartFrog Books.

*To Skip and the many dogs
that I have loved.*

In 1901, Theodore Roosevelt became the 26th president of the United States.

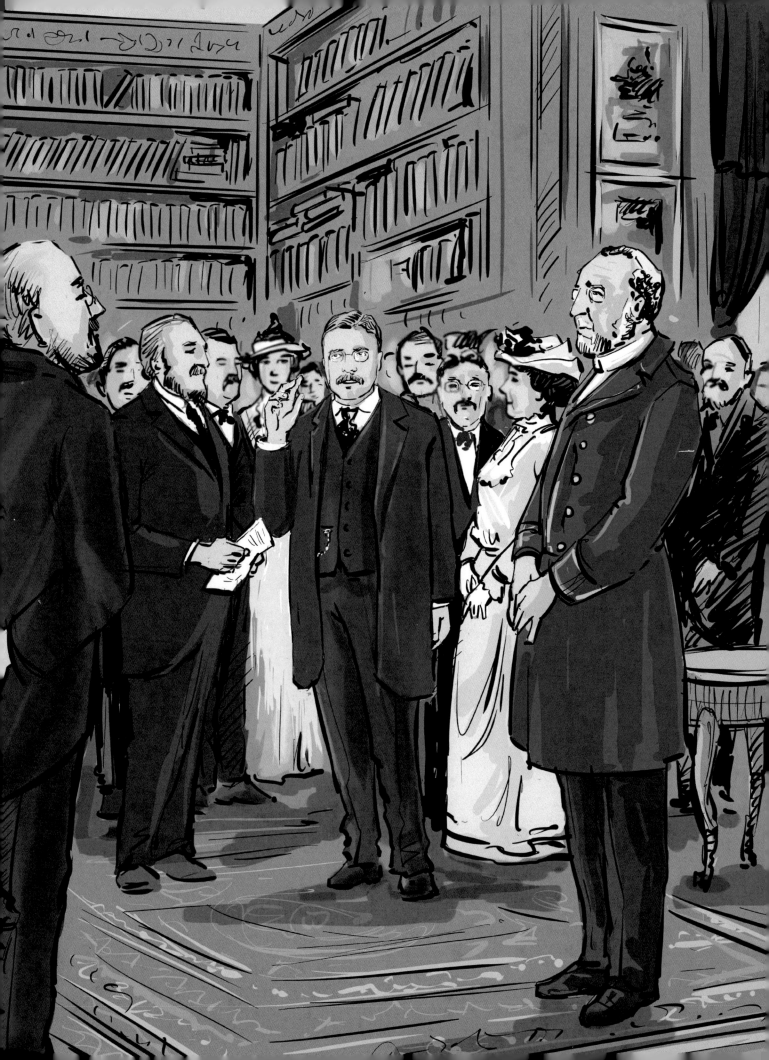

He arrived in Washington, DC, with his wife, 2 daughters, 4 sons, and 43 family pets:

12 horses

1 pony

10 dogs

2 cats

6 guinea pigs

1 lizard

1 snake

1 pig
1 small bear
1 badger
1 blue macaw
2 hens
1 rabbit
1 one-legged rooster
1 parrot
1 barn owl
and Archie's pet rat
named Jonathan.

Mrs. Roosevelt inspected their new house
from basement to attic.
She opened doors and windows.

She cleaned floors, closets, and cabinets.
She made a place for each person and every pet.

One animal had not been invited —
a big Rat. Annie O'Rourke, the cook,
saw it first. She jumped on a stool and
yelled, "There's a rat in the kitchen!"

Archie heard her shout. First, he checked on Jonathan, who was snoozing in his pocket.

Then Archie ran to the President's office. "There's a rat in the kitchen! It's not Jonathan. It's a big nasty rat."

The President was bent over his desk writing on the new White House stationery. He pointed to the stacks and stacks of letters. He told Archie that the rat would have to wait.

Archie told Annie that the President had work to do.

Two mornings later, as Annie was cleaning up
the breakfast dishes, she saw two rats.
She shrieked and threw a bowl
of hominy at them.
"Now it's a pair of rats," she told Archie.

Archie tiptoed down the hall and peeked in on his father.

President Roosevelt was meeting with Booker T. Washington, the most important black leader in the United States.

Archie closed the door. He knew
the rats would have to wait.

Several days later, Annie left a batch of Fat Rascals, her very best biscuits, on the table.

When she came back, they were gone. Archie followed a trail of crumbs and found — five rats! Annie threw a rolling pin at them. "Out of my kitchen!"

Archie rushed to the President's office.
"Five rats!"
The President was pointing at a large globe.
He had to decide where to dig a great canal
joining the Atlantic and Pacific Oceans.
Archie knew the rats would have to wait.

On a cool October day, Annie was baking sugar wafers when she saw beady eyes watching her. She counted them. Fourteen eyes.

Annie raced to Archie's room.
"Seven rats," puffed Annie.

"Gee willikers," said Archie. He ran to the President's office. President Roosevelt was meeting with coal mine owners and workers. The President wanted to make sure the people who dug up the coal got a "square deal." He told the owners to pay a fair wage and to shorten the workday from ten to nine hours.

Otherwise, the miners would refuse to work. Coal was burned for heat, and the President had to make sure that American homes stayed warm in the winter. Archie's shoulders slumped. The rats would have to wait.

A week later, during a family dinner, a rat dashed across the floor. All the Roosevelts jumped up and chased it around the dining room.

"No rats!" yelled Annie. She swatted at it with her broom.

The next morning, a group of men arrived at the White House. Archie thought they had come to catch the rats. But they were here to ask the President to create National Parks for all Americans to enjoy. Archie knew the rats would have to wait.

Several weeks later, Annie counted thirteen rats.

She hurried upstairs to tell Archie.
"The President's hunting bears
in Mississippi," he told her.
Annie sighed. The rats would have to wait.

On his hunt, the President found only a bear cub, which he refused to shoot. Newspaper cartoons showed the President with the little bear. A toy company made stuffed bears and called them Teddy Bears, after the President.

Many, many people
sent Teddy Bears
to the White House.
Mrs. Roosevelt found
a place for each one.

But soon the bears began to sag.
"The rats!" said Archie. "They're taking
the stuffing to make nests."

"These rats have to go," said
the Roosevelt children.
They marched to the President's office.

The President was meeting with railroad owners. He whispered to his family that the owners were charging their customers too much money.

His plan was to talk softly, but carry
a big stick to make sure the railroad
owners treated the customers fairly.
Archie knew that his father wasn't going to hit anyone
with a big stick. The President meant that he would
be angry if the railroad owners didn't agree.

That gave Archie had an idea. He found big sticks for his brothers and sisters, and they banged them all around the kitchen. The rats darted away.

A few days later, the rats were back.
And there were too many to count.
Rats snacked in the kitchen and
scurried along the halls. They nibbled
papers and gnawed on books.
"That's a pack of rats," said Annie.
"It's a mischief of rats," said
Archie. "They have to go."
But President Roosevelt was running
for re-election. He had to travel across
the country and speak to voters.
The rats would have to wait.

When President Roosevelt won re-election, Mrs. Roosevelt, the children, and Annie were happy. They loved everything about living in the White House — except the rats. A few days later, President Roosevelt picked up his hunting gear. The children squealed with excitement. "Are you going to shoot the rats?" The President shook his head no. He was going to hunt big game in Colorado. Archie sighed. The rats would have to wait.

Three weeks later, the President wrote that he had met a terrier named Skip. He believed Skip would be a perfect dog for Archie. What kind of terrier, wondered Archie. When his father returned, Archie met him at the door. Archie had never seen a terrier like Skip, but he liked him right away.

He took Skip to the kitchen to meet Annie.
A rat darted across the room.
"Rat!" said Archie.
Skip's nose twitched. The hair on his back stood
up as stiff as a comb, and his tail quivered.
Skip barked and chased the rat. The
rat ran straight out the door.

But there was another rat. And another. The terrier sprinted from room to room — hunting rats. Rats jumped out the windows and scrambled out the doors. Soon not a rat remained in the White House.

"Wow," said Archie. "Skip's not just a terrier. He's a rat terrier."
"He's a Teddy Roosevelt Terrier," said Annie, tossing Skip a biscuit. President Roosevelt grinned.

About the Author

Judith Tabler grew up a few miles from Theodore Roosevelt's house, Sagamore Hill, in Oyster Bay, New York. She often walked the grounds and visited the Pet Cemetery, where Skip is buried. She is a member of the Theodore Roosevelt Association and has lectured on Roosevelt family life on Long Island. She has written books, picture books, and magazine articles - many about dogs and horses. She now lives outside Washington, DC with her husband and three terriers. You can learn more about her at www.JudithTabler.com.

About Skip

Skip was a real dog, and he was beloved by the Roosevelts—especially by Archie. Much of the story is based on true events. Skip is buried in the Pet Cemetery at the Theodore Roosevelt home, Sagamore Hill, in Oyster Bay, New York. You can learn more about Skip and see more photographs of him at the author's website: www.JudithTabler.com.

Skip with Archie Roosevelt
(Pach Brothers, photographer. (1907). Retrieved from the Library of Congress, https://www.loc.gov/item/2009631484/.)

Notes

Page 4: "*In 1901, Theodore Roosevelt became...*"
In 1900, Theodore Roosevelt was elected to serve as President William McKinley's Vice President. McKinley was shot in Buffalo, New York and died on September 14, 1901. Roosevelt then became the 26th and, at age 42, the youngest President of the United States.

Page 6-7: *"He arrived in Washington, DC,.."*
Members of President Roosevelt's family in the year 1901:

President Theodore Roosevelt, Jr., born October 27, 1858 (age 43)
His wife: Edith Kermit Carow Roosevelt, born August 6, 1861 (age 40)
Children:
Alice Lee Roosevelt, born February 12, 1884 (age 17)
Theodore "Ted" Roosevelt III, born September 13, 1887 (age 14)
Kermit Roosevelt, born October 10, 1889 (age 12)
Ethel Carow Roosevelt, born August 13, 1891 (age 10)
Archibald Bulloch "Archie" Roosevelt, born April 10, 1894 (age 7)
Quentin Roosevelt, born November 19, 1897 (age 4)

The animals:
3 carriage horses (Admiral, General and Judge)[1]
9 riding horses (Bleistein, Renown, Roswell, Rusty, Jocko, Root, Grey Dawn, Wyoming, Yangenka)[2] [3]
1 pony (Algonquin)[4]
10 dogs: Rollo (Saint Bernard),[5] Sailor Boy (Chesapeake Bay Retriever),[6] Gem (unknown breed),[7] Susan (unknown breed, but turned out to be a male after it was named),[8] Allan (Kermit's terrier),[9] Pete (Bull terrier), Brier (unknown breed),[10] Hector (unknown breed)[11] and Black Jack, also called "Jack" (Kermit's Manchester terrier)[12]

[after this dog died they named another dog Jack][13]
2 cats: (Tom Quartz[14] and Slippers [15] [16])
6 guinea pigs (Admiral Dewey, Dewey Jr., Dr. Johnson, Bishop Doane, Fighting Bob Evans, and Father O'Grady)[17] [18]
1 lizard (Bill, "a little live lizard, called a horned frog")[19]
1 snake (Emily Spinach, a green snake belonging to Alice Roosevelt)[20]
1 pig (Maude)[21]
1 small bear (Jonathan Edwards)[22]
1 badger (Josiah)[23] [24]
1 blue macaw (Eli Yale)[25]
1 rabbit (Peter)[26]
2 hens (Baron Spreckle and Fierce)[27]
1 one-legged rooster[28]
1 parrot[29] [30]
1 barn owl (Moses)[31]
1 piebald rat named Jonathan[32]

Page 10: *"She cleaned floors, closets, . ."*
Edith Roosevelt reorganized the president's house to accommodate her large family. She moved all the offices into the newly built West Wing.[33]

Page 17: *"The President was bent over his desk. . ."*
Theodore Roosevelt gave the president's residence the official name of the White House when he ordered stationery with that heading. Before that time, people had called it The Presidential Palace, The Executive Mansion, or The White House.[34]

Page 18: *"Archie told Annie that . . ."*
"The children were strictly trained not to interrupt business."[35]

Page 20: *"She shrieked and threw . . ."*
"Hominy was a staple at the Roosevelt table. In addition to being part of breakfast, it was often served as a starch at lunch and dinner, with meat gravy over it."[36]

Page 24: *"President Roosevelt was meeting with Booker T. Washington..."*
Booker T. Washington met and dined with Theodore Roosevelt on
October 16, 1901. He was the first black man to dine with a president. The
event was front page news throughout the United States.[37]

Page 28: *"Several days later, Annie left a batch of..."*
Recipe for Fat Rascals:
> 4 cups flour
> Salt (a pinch? no exact amount given)
> ¼ cup sugar
> 4 teaspoons baking powder
> Mix well.
> Cut in 1 ½ cups butter.
> Then stir in 1 pound dried currants.
> Mix well again.
> Add 1 cup milk, little by little.
> With each addition, mix with a fork until a soft dough forms. Roll the
> dough approximately ½ inch thick on a lightly floured board. Use a
> 2-inch round cutter to shape the biscuits.
> Bake biscuits on an ungreased cookie sheet in a hot (450° F) oven for
> about 12 minutes, until nicely brown.
> When done, remove, split and butter each biscuit, and serve piping
> hot.
> Makes approximately 3 dozen biscuits. [38]

Page 32: *"He had to decide where to dig..."*
President McKinley had supported the building of a canal in Nicaragua
to link the Atlantic and Pacific Oceans. Theodore Roosevelt preferred to
locate the canal in Panama. Roosevelt persuaded Congress to agree with
him, citing volcanic activity in Nicaragua.[39]

Page 34: *"On a cool October day, Annie was baking..."*
Recipe for Annie's Sugar Wafers:

1 cup butter
1 teaspoon vanilla
⅔ cup sugar
2 eggs
Flour (cake)
Cream 1 cup butter until light and fluffy.
Add 1 teaspoon vanilla.
Gradually beat in ⅔ cup sugar and 2 well-beaten eggs.
Stir in 1 ½ cups cake flour. (Regular flour may be used, but the cookies will not be as delicate.)
Mix well and drop by teaspoonfuls on a cookie sheet.
Spread thin with a knife dipped in cold water.
Bake in a hot (375° F) oven for about 8 minutes.
Makes 5 dozen.[40]

Page 38: *"President Roosevelt was meeting with coal mine owners. . ."*
Roosevelt used the term "square deal" to describe the settlement of a mining strike in October 1902. Roosevelt felt that he had reached a fair compromise for both sides of the disagreement.

Page 40: *"All the Roosevelts jumped up . . ."*
"In the old days, it was no uncommon thing for a rat or a mouse to present himself in the dining-room at mealtimes. During the Roosevelt Administration, I remember at least two occasions when the family dinner party was broken up to chase a rat around the room. It was great sport for the male members of the family, the President included."[41]

Page 42: *"The next morning, a group of men arrived. . ."*
In 1902, the Wind River Cave in South Dakota was surveyed and designated a United States National Park the following year, on January 3, 1903.

Page 48: *"A toy company made stuffed bears..."*
Clifford Berryman drew a cartoon of President Roosevelt and the bear for the *Washington Post* on November 16, 1902. This gave a New York candy store owner, Morris Michtom, an idea. His wife made stuffed bears, and they called them "Teddy's bears." The rapid popularity of these bears led Michtom to mass-produce them as Teddy Bears. The company evolved into the Ideal Novelty and Toy Company."[42] The author admits there is no factual evidence of the rats taking Teddy Bear stuffing for nests. Theodore Roosevelt's friends and family never called him Teddy. In his childhood, he was "Teedie." As an adult, he preferred people to address him with his initials "TR" or by his military rank "Colonel."

Page 56: *"The President was meeting with railroad owners...."*
The Northern Securities Corporation was called a trust, because it managed many railroad companies. This trust was so big that no other railroad companies could compete with it. That meant that the Northern Securities Corporation could charge very high prices for anyone using their trains. In 1904, President Roosevelt said that this was unfair. The Supreme Court agreed and stated that the Northern Securities Corporation violated the Sherman Anti-Trust Act. The Northern Securities Corporation was forced to break apart so that independent, smaller railroad companies could form. Then the customer could choose which railroad provided the best service and value. Americans gave Roosevelt the nickname: "Trust Buster."

Page 57: *"His plan was to talk softly, but carry..."*
"Speak softly and carry a big stick; you will go far" is an African proverb that Roosevelt liked. He first wrote it in a letter when he was Governor of New York on January 26, 1900. He used the phrase to explain how he convinced politicians to agree with him. His oratory would be calm, but everyone understood that he had the power to reinforce his position. Later, as president, Roosevelt repeated the phrase to show how he dealt with problems.[43]

Page 60: *"It's a mischief of rats..."*
The collective noun for rats is a mischief.

Page 62: *"When President Roosevelt won..."*
Theodore Roosevelt often called himself the "accidental president" until he was elected in his own right as President of the United States on November 8, 1904.

Page 64: *"Three weeks later..."*
"There is a very cunning little dog named Skip, belonging to John Goff's pack, who has completely adopted me. I think I shall take him home to Archie. He likes to ride on Dr. Lambert's horse, or mine, and though he is not as big as Jack, takes eager part in the fight with every bear and bobcat."[44]

Page 70: *"Wow," said Archie...."*
President Roosevelt is credited with giving this newly evolved, American version of the British Feist Terrier its new name: the Rat Terrier."[45] Years later, Theodore Roosevelt wrote that another terrier, Scamp, was the best ratter in the household.[46] But Skip had been the first. Today, two dog breeds - the Rat Terrier and the Teddy Roosevelt Terrier - recognize that the popularity of Skip influenced the establishment of their breeds.

Endnotes

1   "Our Lively Capital," *The Deseret News*, Salt Lake City, November 9, 1901, 17.

2   Roosevelt, Theodore. Joseph Bucklin Bishop, editor. *Theodore Roosevelt's Letters to His Children*. New York: Cosimo Classics, 2006. Letter to Ted, May 7, 1901, 27.

3   Roosevelt. *Theodore Roosevelt's Letters to His Children*. Letter to Kermit, Nov. 28, 1902, 37-38.

4   Roosevelt. *Theodore Roosevelt's Letters to His Children*. Letter to James A. Garfield, Dec. 26, 1902, 38-40.

5   Theodore Roosevelt and Rollo. Item Identifier: Roosevelt Class No. 560.52 190x Shelfmark TRC-PH-3, photograph, Ritzmann, Charles L., photographer, Date: ca. 1905-1909, Roosevelt with a Saint Bernard, White House in the background, Washington (D.C.). Photograph by Charles L. Ritzmann. Theodore Roosevelt Collection, Harvard College Library.

6   Roosevelt, Theodore. *The Autobiography of Theodore Roosevelt*, 1913, reprint Seven Treasure's Publications, 2009, 190.

7   Roosevelt. *Theodore Roosevelt's Letters to His Children*. Letter to Kermit, October 13, 1902, 35-36.

8   Roosevelt, *Autobiography of Theodore Roosevelt*. 190.

9   Roosevelt. *Theodore Roosevelt's Letters to His Children*. Letter to Mrs. Douglas Robinson, December 25, 1903, 81.

10 Roosevelt. *Theodore Roosevelt's Letters to His Children*. Letter to Kermit, November 15, 1903, 75.

11 Roosevelt. *Theodore Roosevelt's Letters to His Children*. Letter to Kermit, November 15, 1903, 75.

12 Roosevelt. *Theodore Roosevelt's Letters to His Children*. Letter to Ted, May 31, 1901, 31-32.

13 Roosevelt. *Theodore Roosevelt's Letters to His Children*. Letter to Kermit, December 17, 1904, 110-111.

14 Roosevelt. *Theodore Roosevelt's Letters to His Children*. Letter to Kermit, January 6, 1903, 41.

15 Quentin (?) and cat "Slippers"(?) on board the Mayflower. Roosevelt Class No. 570.R67q. Roosevelt family photographs copied from albums at Sagamore Hill (Roosevelt R500.R67). Theodore Roosevelt Collection: Harvard College Library.

16 Roosevelt. *Theodore Roosevelt's Letters to His Children*. Letter to Quentin, April 1, 1906, 157.

17 Roosevelt. *Theodore Roosevelt's Letters to His Children*. Letter to E.S. Martin, November 22, 1900, 18-19.

18 Roosevelt. *Theodore Roosevelt's Letters to His Children*. Letter to Ted, May 7, 1901, 27.

19 Roosevelt. *Theodore Roosevelt's Letters to His Children*. Letter to Archie, May 10, 1903, 47-48.

20 Green Chain a Snake: Remarkable Living Ornament of Miss Roosevelt. *The Washington Post* (1877-1922); Aug 14, 1904, A2; ProQuest Historical Newspapers: *The Washington Post*.

21 Roosevelt. *Theodore Roosevelt's Letters to His Children*. Letter to Ethel, Jan. 29, 1901, 24-25.

22 Roosevelt. *Theodore Roosevelt's Letters to His Children*. Letter to E.S. Martin, November 22, 1900, 18-19.

23 Roosevelt. *Theodore Roosevelt's Letters to His Children*. Letter to E.S. Martin, November 22, 1900, 18-19.

24 Roosevelt, *Autobiography of Theodore Roosevelt*, 190.

25 Roosevelt. *Theodore Roosevelt's Letters to His Children*. Letter to Joel Chandler Harris, June 9, 1902, 35.

26 Roosevelt. *Theodore Roosevelt's Letters to His Children*. Letter to Kermit, May 28, 1904, 96-97.

27 Roosevelt. *Theodore Roosevelt's Letters to His Children*. Letter to Emily Carow, August 6, 1903, 50.

28 Theodore Roosevelt's pet one-legged rooster. [1910 -1920?] Image. Retrieved from the Library of Congress, https://www.loc.gov/item/2010645533/. (Accessed August 04, 2016).

29 Alice Roosevelt Longworth with parrot. Photograph by Pach Brothers. Shelfmark TRC-PH-2. Roosevelt Class No. 570.R67al, Theodore Roosevelt Collection Photographs: Family Portraits. Theodore Roosevelt Collection, Harvard College Library.

30 Roosevelt. *Theodore Roosevelt's Letters to His Children*. Letter to Ted, November 28, 1903, 80-81.

31 Theodore Roosevelt Collection photographs: Roosevelt-Rondon Scientific Expedition, 1913-1914. MS Am 3069. Houghton Library, Harvard University, Cambridge, Mass. Repository Harvard University Library, Institution Harvard University, Accessed 04 August 2016.

32 Roosevelt. *Theodore Roosevelt's Letters to His Children*. Letter to Joel Chandler Harris, June 9, 1902, 35.

33 Gould, Lewis L. *Edith Kermit Roosevelt: Creating the Modern First Lady*. Lawrence, Kansas: University of Kansas, 2013, 38-42.

34 Hoover, Irwin H. *Forty-Two Years in the White House*. Boston: Houghton Mifflin Company, 1934, 111.

35 Roosevelt. *The Autobiography of Theodore Roosevelt*, 189.

36 Cannon, Poppy and Patricia Brooks. *The Presidents' Cookbook*. New York: Funk and Wagnalls, 1968, 353.

37 Davis, Deborah. *Guest of Honor*, New York: Atria Books, 2012, 1.

38 Cannon, Poppy and Patricia Brooks, *The Presidents' Cookbook*, 357.

39 McCullough, David, The Path Between the Seas. New York: Simon & Schuster, 1977, 270-294.

40 Cannon, Poppy and Patricia Brooks, *The Presidents' Cookbook*, 364 and Anthony, Carl Sferrazza. *America's First Families*. New York: Touchstone, 2000, 56.

41 Hoover, *Forty-two Years in the White House*, 110.

42 The Theodore Roosevelt Association. *Real Teddy Bear Story*. Retrieved from http://www.theodoreroosevelt.org /site /c.elKSIdOWIiJ8H/ b.8684621/k.6632/Real_Teddy_Bear_Story.htm. Also note that Clifford Berryman is most often associated with the *Evening Star* newspaper, but his original Teddy Bear cartoon appeared when he was working for *The Washington Post*.

43 "Speak softly and carry a big stick; you will go far." Letter from Theodore Roosevelt to Henry Sprague, January 26, 1900. Library of Congress. http://www.loc.gov/exhibits/treasures/tr11c.html#obj15

44 Roosevelt. *Theodore Roosevelt's Letters to His Children*. Letter to Kermit, May 12, 1905, 125-126.

45 Kane, Alice J. 2003. *Rat Terrier*. Allenhurst, New Jersey: Kennel Club Books, 13-14 and Tabler, Judith. *Rat Terrier: The Essential Guide for the Rat Terrier Lover*. Neptune City, NJ: TFH, 2010, 9-10.

46 Roosevelt. *Theodore Roosevelt's Letters to His Children*. Letter to Archie, March 8, 1908, 222-223.

Works Cited

Anthony, Carl Sferrazza. 2000. *America's First Families*. New York: Touchstone.

Cannon, Poppy and Patricia Brooks. 1968. *The Presidents' Cookbook; Practical Recipes from George Washington to the Present*. New York: Funk & Wagnalls.

Cook, Blanche Wiesen. 1993. *Eleanor Roosevelt*. Vol. 1. 2 vols. New York: Penguin Books.

Dalton, Kathleen. 2002. *Theodore Roosevelt: A Strenuous Life*. New York: Knopf.

Deseret Times, 1901. "Our Lively Capital." November 9: 17. *Deseret evening news*. (Great Salt Lake City [Utah]). *Chronicling America: Historic American Newspapers*. Lib. of Congress. https://chroniclingamerica.loc.gov/lccn/sn83045555/1901-01-28/ed-1/seq-1/.

Davis, Deborah. 2012. *Guest of Honor*. New York: Atria Books.

Gould, Lewis L. 2013. *Edith Kermit Roosevelt*. Lawrence, Kansas: University of Kansas.

Hagner, Isabella. 2009. *Memoirs of Isabella Hagner 1901-1905*. Edited by Priscille Roosevelt. White House History 26. Fall. Accessed January 10, 2016. http://www.whitehouse history.org/memoirs-the-first-white-house-social-secretary-isabella-hagner.

Hoover, Irwin Hood. 1934. *Forty-two Years in the White House*. Boston: Houghton Mifflin.

Kane, Alice J. 2003. *Rat Terrier*. Allenhurst, New Jersey: Kennel Club Books.

McCullough, David G. 2003. *Mornings on Horseback*. New York: Simon & Schuster.

—. 1977. The Path Between the Seas. New York: Simon & Schuster.

Morris, Edmund. 1979. *The Rise of Theodore Roosevelt*. New York: Coward, McCann & Geoghegan, Inc.

—. 2001. *Theodore Rex*. New York: Random House.

Roosevelt, Theodore. 2012. *A Passion to Lead, Theodore Roosevelt in His Own Words*. Edited by Laura Ross. New York: Sterling Signature.

—. 1913. *The Autobiography of Theodore Roosevelt*. New York: Charles Scribner's and Sons, 2009 Reprint. Seven Treasures Publications.

—. 1919. *Theodore Roosevelt's Letters to His Children*. Edited by Joseph Bucklin Bishop. New York: Charles Scribner's and Sons.

Tabler, Judith. 2010. *Rat Terrier, The Essential Guide for the Rat Terrier Lover*. Neptune City, New Jersey: T.F.H. Publications, Inc.

The Washington Post. 1907. "Arrival at Pine Knot." May 18: 3.

The Washington Post. 1905. "Journey to Denver." May 9: 3.

The Washington Post. 1907. "Pets at the White House: Queer Animals Presented to President and Family." January 22: 18.

The Washington Post. 1905. "President As Host." May 8: 1.

The Washington Post. 1907. "President Home Again." January 1: 1.

The Washington Post. 1905. "Shorty, the Tree-climbing Dog." October 7: S6.

The Washington Post. 1907. "Skip Sick, Archie Sad." April 11: 12.

U.S. National Park Service. Nd. Sagamore Hill National Historical Site. Web. 27 Sept. 2016

U.S. National Park Services. Wind Cave National Park, South Dakota. https://www.nps.gov/wica/learn/historyculture/1902-uswcs-survey.htm.

Other Books about Theodore Roosevelt

For younger readers:

Brown, Don. 2009. *Teedie: The Story of Young Teddy Roosevelt*. New York: HMH Books for Young Readers. 32 pages, ages 4-7.

Keating, Frank. 2006. *Theodore*, New York, Simon & Schuster. 32 pages, ages 6 to 9.

Kimmelman, Leslie, 2009. *Mind Your Manners, Alice Roosevelt*. Atlanta, GA: Peachtree Publishing. 32 pages ages 4 to 8.

Murphy, Frank. 2015. *Take a Hike, Teddy Roosevelt!* New York: Random House Books for Young Readers. 48 pages, ages 5-8.

Rappaport, Doreen. 2013. *To Dare Mighty Things: The Life of Theodore Roosevelt*. White Plains, NY: Disney-Hyperion. 48 pages, ages 6-8.

Rosenstock, Barb. 2012. *The Camping Trip that Changed America: Theodore Roosevelt, John Muir, and Our National Parks*. New York: Dial Books. 32 pages, ages 6-8. Note: This book won the Theodore Roosevelt Association Children's Book Award, 2020.

Sage, James. 2019. *Teddy: The Remarkable Tale of a President, a Cartoonist, a Toymaker and a Bear*. Toronto, Ontario, Canada: Kids Can Press. 40 pages, ages 6 to 9.

Wadsworth, Ginger. 2009. *Camping with the President*. Honesdale, PA: Calkins Creek. 32 pages, ages 9 to 12.

Middle grade and older readers:

Burgan, Michael. 2014. *Who Was Theodore Roosevelt?* New York: Grosset & Dunlap; DGS edition. 112 pages, ages 8-18.

Fritz, Jean. 1991. *Bully for You, Teddy Roosevelt!* New York: Putnam. 127 pages, ages 8-12.

Harness, Cheryl. 2007. *The Remarkable Rough-Riding Life of Theodore Roosevelt and the Rise of Empire America.* Washington, D.C.: National Geographic Children's Books. 144 pages, ages 8-12.

Hollihan, Kerrie Logan. 2010. *Theodore Roosevelt for Kids: His Life and Times, 21 Activities* (For Kids series). Chicago: Chicago Review Press. 144 pages, ages 9-11.

Kerley, Barbara. 2008. *What To Do About Alice?: How Alice Roosevelt Broke the Rules, Charmed the World, and Drove Her Father Teddy Crazy!* New York: Scholastic. 48 pages, ages 7-10.

Kidd, Ronald, 2008. *Teddy Roosevelt and the Treasure of Ursa Major.* Fiction, New York: Aladdin. 128 pages, ages 7 to 10.

Mills, Claudia. 2012. *Being Teddy Roosevelt: A Boy, a President and a Plan.* Fiction. New York: Perfect Learning, Square Fish - reprint. 112 pages, ages 7 to 10.

Monjo, Ferdinand N. 1970. *One Bad Thing About Father.* New York: Harper and Row. 64 pages, ages 9-10.

Schwatrz, Heather E. 2016. *Theodore Roosevelt's Presidency* (Presidential Powerhouses). Minneapolis: Lerner Publishing. 104 pages, ages 12-17.

Seiple, Samantha. 2017. *Death on the River of Doubt: Theodore Roosevelt's Amazon Adventure.* New York: Scholastic. 240 pages, ages 12-17.

Made in the USA
Middletown, DE
15 September 2021